First published in Belgium and Holland by Clavis Uitgeverij, Hasselt – Amsterdam, 2015
Copyright © 2015, Clavis Uitgeverij

English translation from the Dutch by Clavis Publishing Inc. New York
Copyright © 2016 for the English language edition: Clavis Publishing Inc. New York

Visit us on the web at www.clavisbooks.com

Vroom! Kevin's Big Book of Cars written by and illustrated by Liesbet Slegers
Original title: *Vroem! Het grote autoboek van Karel*
Translated from the Dutch by Clavis Publishing

ISBN 978-1-60537-257-0

This book was printed in December 2015 at Publikum d.o.o., Slavka Rodica 6, Belgrade, Serbia

First Edition
10 9 8 7 6 5 4 3 2 1

Liesbet Slegers

Vroom!
Kevin's Big Book of Vehicles

Clavis

NEW YORK

Hello, I'm Kevin. I like playing with cars and trucks. With **quick helpers**, like the ambulance and the fire engine.

And with **strong workers**, like the excavator and the crane.

But most of all, I like playing with the tractor. On the farm, the tractor and the farmer do all the hard work.

Vroom! Watch out for that fast race car!

Will you come for a ride with me through this book?

On the road

Vroom! Bear, will you ride with me?
Bumping along the roads
is fun, you'll see!

Stop!
Can you see those feet?
It's someone
trying to cross the street.

There are many kinds of vehicles.
They can travel on a regular road or on a highway.
They can take you to school, to work, or on a journey.

Kevin's dad is filling up the car.
What other vehicles do you know?
And which one never has to refuel?

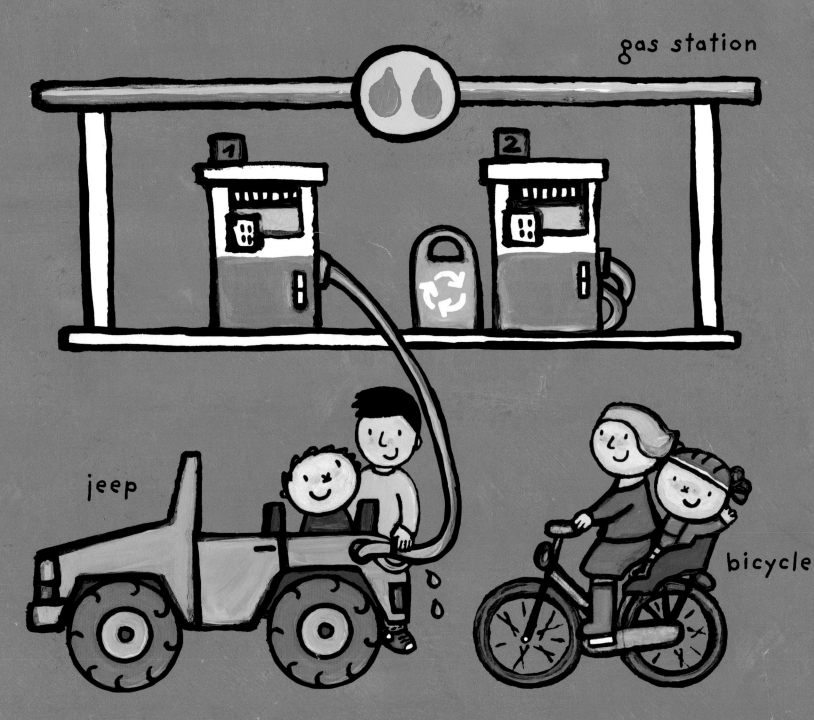

gas station

jeep

bicycle

truck

motorcycle

scooter

bus

van

Kevin's mom has such a nice car!
Kevin can name many parts of the car:
the engine, the windshield wiper...

What parts do you know?

windshield wiper

taillight

gas tank cover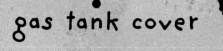

door

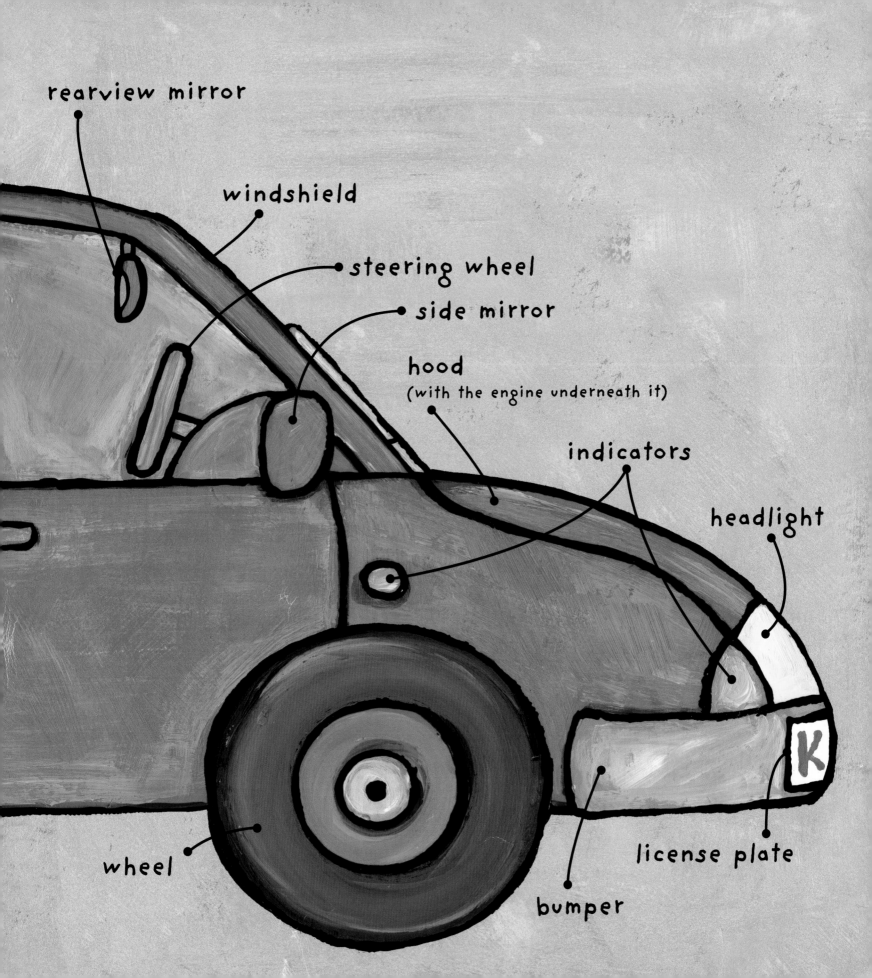

Which vehicle needs tracks? And which one can ride on the road?
Can you find Kevin, Katie, Ali, and their other friends?
Which vehicles are they driving?

bus

truck

tracks

cold storage truck

moving truck

milk truck

horse trailer

car carrier trailer

Quick helpers

Weew-weew, can you hear the siren?
Weew-weew, get out of the way!
We have to take care of Rabbit.
He's been wounded, but he will be okay.

Look! These cars come to help. They arrive quickly with their flashing lights and their sirens. The ambulance, the fire engine, the police car... it's a good thing they exist!
Can you name all these vehicles?
And which car doesn't belong here?

tow truck

Tow trucks pull vehicles that can't drive anymore. Or, together with the police, they tow away cars that are parked in the wrong spot.

police car

police motorcycle

ambulance

zoo van

fire engine

police van

When he grows up, Kevin wants to be a firefighter.
Can you see all the things on the side of the page?
Can you find them in the fire engine?
Which of these things does a firefighter not use?

fire
extinguisher

ball

ax

banana

gloves

bear

The three quick helpers get an emergency call.

Where does each car need to go?
And which one needs to go to two places?

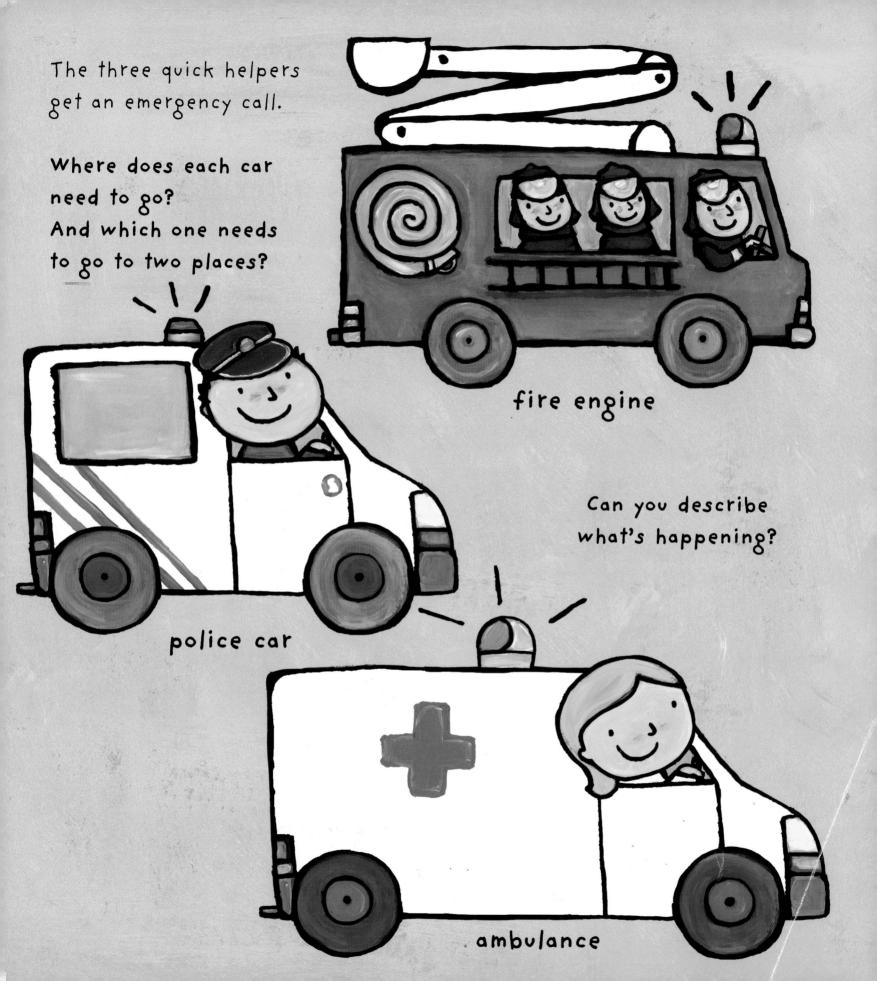

fire engine

Can you describe what's happening?

police car

ambulance

A house is on fire.

A girl has fallen and hurt herself.

The traffic lights are broken.

A thief tries to escape.

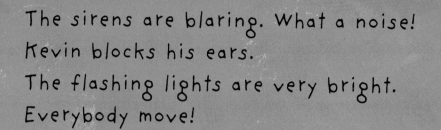

The sirens are blaring. What a noise!
Kevin blocks his ears.
The flashing lights are very bright.
Everybody move!

What sounds can you hear on the road?
Can you make those sounds, too?

weew-
weew

rrrriing

Ambulance driver Kevin

Weew-weew!
"Everybody move!
Bear is hurt!"
police officer Katie says.
The cars have to stop
because ambulance driver Kevin
is approaching fast
with his flashing lights.

Bear fell off the table and has a headache.
Quick, take him to the hospital!

"Hang in there, Bear!" Kevin says. "I will take you to a doctor.
He will help you."

In the hospital, Bear is treated really well.
After a little while, he goes home to his cuddly friends.
And at night, he sleeps in Kevin's cozy bed again!

Strong workers that build things
(and construct roads)

Backhoe digs backward
and drives every which way.
We have lots of work
to do today.

Digging, moving
a mountain of sand.
We are working
really hard.
Do you understand?

On construction sites or on the road,
you can sometimes see
strong vehicles working.

Have you ever seen them?
What are they doing?
Which vehicle on the right
doesn't belong there? Why not?

Kevin is sitting in the strong bulldozer.
It clears sand and rocks.

crane

garbage
truck

ice-cream truck

grapple
truck

Kevin loves playing outside.
He digs a hole in the sand
with his shovel.

And there are many vehicles
that **dig in the sand.**

In the place where they want to build a house,
the **backhoe** does the same thing that Kevin does.
Super fast, it digs a big, deep pit
in the sand. What a **strong worker!**

The sand from the pit goes into a **dump truck** that takes it away.

The big concrete mixer **pours** a layer of **concrete**.
The **mixer** is always spinning,
which keeps the concrete soft and liquid.

The construction workers
make sure the concrete
forms a smooth surface.
After a while, the concrete
becomes as hard as rock.
It's so strong, you can build
a house or construct a road
on top of it.

The **garbage truck** keeps
everything nice and clean.
It picks up the trash bags.
That's a big job.

The **street sweeper** cleans the streets.
All the garbage must go!

Workers use a **cherry picker**
to replace a streetlamp.
There you go, now there's light again.

A house made of blocks

"Will you help me build, Katie?" Kevin asks.
"Look, my blocks are the bricks."
They are building a big house for Bear and Rabbit.
Together, they are piling up the blocks.
Kevin builds a really big tower, bigger than himself!
The tower is the chimney of the house. Make sure it doesn't fall!

"Look," Katie says, "this shoebox can be the garage.
That's where I'll put Bear and Rabbit's car."
"And Mommy's plant can be the tree near the house," Kevin laughs.

"Hey, where are my shoes?" someone asks.
It's Daddy.
"Ah, I see... the shoebox," Daddy says.
"Wait! My feet won't fit in the car that's inside of it..."
Kevin and Katie laugh. Daddy is funny!

Do you see his two shoes?

Strong workers
on the farm

Bucket, shovel, Bear,
We drive around here and there
In the tractor that's so strong!
Back and forth in the field,
we work hard and we work long.

On the farm, the farmer cannot do
without his tractor.
It can pull a cart or a trailer or a plow.

Kevin loves to ride along.

cart

plow

tractor

Hmm, Kevin is eating a sandwich.
It's made of wheat.

Where does wheat come from?

The grain grows in the field. When it's ready,
the farmer mows it with the **combine harvester**,
the biggest and strongest vehicle on the farm.
The farmer also needs a **tractor**.

1. The wheat is **cut**.

3. The grain is moved through a long pipe into the trailer that is attached to the tractor.

2. In the combine, the wheat grain is separated from the plant. That is called **threshing**.

Look at all those wheels. They are all different.
Do you know which vehicle they belong to?

tractor

wheelbarrow

cart

bicycle

Kevin is at the farm.
Can you find him?
But... what a funny farm!

Which vehicles don't belong here?
And where do they belong?

Hello, we are Kevin and Katie.
We are in a hurry.
No time to talk.
We're riding in our car.
Whoosh, we pass you by.
Would you like to ride along?
We are going really far!